SNOW STORM

Alexander Pushkin

translated by Sutherland Edwards

first published in 1892

Towards the end of 1811, at a memorable period for Russians, lived on his own domain of Nenaradova the kind-hearted Gravril R. He was celebrated in the whole district for his hospitality and his genial character. Neighbours constantly visited him to have something to eat and drink, and to play at five-copeck boston with his wife, Praskovia. Some, too, went to have a look at their daughter, Maria; a tall pale girl of seventeen. She was an heiress, and they desired her either for themselves or for their sons.

Maria had been brought up on French novels, and consequently was in love. The object of her affection was a poor ensign in the army, who was now at home in his small village on leave of absence. As a matter of course, the young man reciprocated Maria's passion. But the parents of his beloved, noticing their mutual attachment, forbade their daughter even to think of him, while they received him worse than an ex-assize judge.

Our lovers corresponded, and met alone daily in the pine wood or by the old roadway chapel. There they vowed everlasting love, inveighed against fate, and exchanged various suggestions. Writing and talking in this way, they quite naturally reached the following conclusion:--

If we cannot exist
apart from each
other, and if the
tyranny of hard-
hearted parents
throws obstacles
in the way of our
happiness, then
can we not manage
without them?

Of course, this happy
idea originated in
the mind of the

young man; but it pleased the romantic imagination of Maria immensely.

Winter set in and put a stop to their meetings. But their correspondence became all the more active. Vladimir begged Maria in every letter to give herself up to him that they might get married secretly, hide for a while, and then throw themselves at the feet of the parents, who would of course in the end be touched by their heroic constancy and say to them, "Children, come to our arms!"

Maria hesitated a long while, and out of many different plans proposed, that of flight was for a time rejected. At last, however, she consented. On the appointed day she was to decline supper, and retire to her room under the plea of a headache. She and her maid, who was in the secret, were then to go out into the garden by the back stairs, and beyond the garden they would find a sledge ready for them, would get into it and drive a distance of five miles from Nenaradova, to the village of Jadrino, straight to the church, where Vladimir would be waiting for them.

On the eve of the decisive day, Maria did not sleep all night; she was packing and tying up linen and dresses. She wrote, moreover, a long letter to a friend of hers, a sentimental young lady; and another to her parents. Of the latter, she took leave in the most touching terms. She excused the step she was taking by reason of the unconquerable power of love, and wound up by declaring that she should consider it the happiest moment of her life when she was allowed to throw herself at the feet of her dearest parents. Sealing both letters with a Toula seal, on which were engraven two flaming hearts with an appropriate inscription, she at last threw herself upon her bed before daybreak and dozed off, though even then she was awake tied from one moment to another by terrible thoughts. First it seemed to her that at the moment of entering the sledge in order to go and get married her father stopped her, and with cruel rapidity dragged her over the snow and threw her into a dark bottomless cellar, down which she fell headlong with an indescribable sinking of the heart. Then she saw Vladimir, lying on the grass, pale and bleeding; with his dying breath he implored her to make haste and marry him. Other hideous and senseless visions floated before her one after another. Finally she rose paler than usual, and with, a real headache.

Both her father and her mother remarked her indisposition. Their tender anxiety and constant inquiries, "What is the matter with you, Maria--are you ill?" cut her to the heart. She tried to pacify them and to appear cheerful; but she could not. Evening set in. The idea that she was passing the day for the last time in the midst of her family oppressed her. In her secret heart she took leave of everybody, of everything which surrounded her.

Supper was served; her heart beat violently. In a trembling voice she declared that she did not want any supper, and wished her father and mother good-night. They kissed her, and as usual blessed her; and she nearly wept.

Reaching her own room she threw herself into an easy chair and burst into tears. Her maid begged her to be calm and take courage. Everything was ready. In half-an-hour Maria would leave for ever her parents' house, her own room, her peaceful life as a young girl.

Out of doors the snow

was falling, the wind howling. The shutters rattled and shook. In everything she seemed to recognise omens and threats.

Soon the whole home was quiet and asleep. Maria wrapped herself in a shawl, put on a warm cloak, and with a box in her hand passed out on to the back staircase. The maid carried two bundles after her. They descended into the garden. The snowstorm raged: a strong wind blew against them as if trying to stop the young culprit. With difficulty they reached the end of the garden. In the road a sledge awaited them.

The horses from cold would not stand still. Vladimir's coachman

was walking to and
fro in front of them,
trying to quiet them.
He helped the young
lady and her maid
to their seats, and
packing away the
bundles and the
dressing-case took
up the reins, and the
horses flew forward
into the darkness of
the night.

    *   *   *   *

Having entrusted the young lady to the care of fate and of Tereshka the coachman, let us return to the young lover.

Vladimir had spent the whole day in driving. In the morning he had called on the Jadrino priest, and, with difficulty, came to terms with him. Then he went to seek for witnesses from amongst the neighbouring gentry. The first on whom he called was a former cornet of horse, Dravin by name, a man in his forties, who consented at once. The adventure, he declared, reminded him of old times and of his larks when he was in the Hussars. He persuaded Vladimir to stop to dinner with him, assuring him that there would be no difficulty in getting the other two witnesses. Indeed, immediately after dinner in came the surveyor Schmidt, with a moustache and spurs, and the son of a captain-magistrate, a boy of sixteen, who had recently entered the Uhlans. They not only accepted Vladimir's proposal, but even swore that they were ready to sacrifice their lives for him. Vladimir embraced them with delight, and drove off to get everything ready.

It had long been dark. Vladimir despatched his trustworthy Tereshka to Nenaradova with his two-horsed sledge, and with appropriate instructions for the occasion. For himself he ordered the small sledge with one horse, and started alone without a coachman for Jadrino, where Maria ought to arrive in a couple of hours. He knew the road, and the drive would only occupy twenty minutes.

But Vladimir had scarcely passed from

the enclosure into the open field when the wind rose, and soon there was a driving snowstorm so heavy and so severe that he could not see. In a moment the road was covered with snow. All landmarks disappeared in the murky yellow darkness, through which fell white flakes of snow. Sky and earth became merged into one. Vladimir, in the midst of the field, tried in vain to get to the road. The horse walked on at random, and every moment stepped either into deep snow or into a rut, so that the sledge was constantly upsetting. Vladimir tried at least not to lose the right direction; but it seemed to him that more than half an hour had passed, and he had not yet reached the Jadrino wood. Another ten minutes passed, and still the wood was invisible. Vladimir drove across fields intersected by deep ditches. The snowstorm did not abate, and the sky did not clear. The horse was getting tired and the perspiration rolled from him like hail, in spite of the fact that every moment his legs were disappearing in the snow.

At last Vladimir found that he was going in the wrong direction. He stopped; began to reflect, recollect, and consider; till at last he became convinced that he ought to have turned to the right. He did so now. His horse could scarcely drag along. But he had been more than an hour on the road, and Jadrino could not now be far. He drove and drove, but there was no getting out of the field. Still snow-drifts and ditches. Every moment the sledge was upset, and every moment Vladimir had to raise it up.

Time was slipping by, and Vladimir grew seriously anxious. At last in the distance some dark object could be seen.

Vladimir turned in its direction, and as he drew near found it was a wood.

"Thank Heaven," he thought, "I am now near the end."

He drove by the side of the wood, hoping to come at once upon the familiar road, or, if not, to pass round the wood. Jadrino was situated immediately behind it.

He soon found the road, and passed into the darkness of the wood, now stripped by the winter. The wind could not rage here; the road was smooth, the horse picked up courage, and Vladimir was comforted.

He drove and drove, but still Jadrino was not to be seen; there was no end to the wood. Then to his horror he discovered that he had got into a strange wood. He was in despair. He whipped his horse, and the poor animal started off at a trot. But it soon got tired, and in a quarter of an hour, in spite of all poor Vladimir's efforts, could only crawl.

Gradually the trees became thinner, and Vladimir drove out of the wood, but Jadrino was not to be seen. It must have been about midnight. Tears gushed from the young man's eyes. He drove on at random; and now the weather abated, the clouds dispersed, and before him was a wide stretch of plain, covered with a white billowy carpet. The night was comparatively clear, and he could see a small village a short distance off, which consisted of four or five cottages. Vladimir drove towards it.

At the first door he jumped out of the sledge, ran up to the window, and tapped. After a few minutes a wooden, shutter was raised, and an old man stuck out his grey beard.

"What do you want?"

"How far is Jadrino?"

"How far is Jadrino?"

"Yes, yes! Is it far?"

"Not far; about ten miles."

At this answer Vladimir clutched hold of his hair, and stood motionless, like a man condemned to death.

"Where do you come from?" added the man. Vladimir had not the courage to reply.

"My man," he said, "can you procure me

horses to Jadrino?"

"We have no horses," answered the peasant.

"Could I find a guide? I will pay him any sum he likes."

"Stop!" said the old man, dropping the shutter; "I will send my son out to you; he will conduct you."

Vladimir waited.

Scarcely a minute had passed when he again knocked. The shutter was lifted and a beard was seen.

"What do you want?"

"What about your son?"

"He'll come out directly: he is putting on his boots. Are you cold? Come in and warm yourself."

"Thanks! Send out your son quickly."

The gate creaked; a youth came out with a cudgel, and walked on in front, at one time pointing out the road, at another looking for it in a mass of drifted snow.

"What o'clock is it?" Vladimir asked him.

"It will soon be

daylight," replied the young-peasant. Vladimir spoke not another word.

The cocks were crowing, and it was light when they reached Jadrino. The church was closed. Vladimir paid the guide, and drove into the yard of the priest's house. In the yard his two-horsed sledge was not to be seen. What news awaited him?

*   *   *   *

 But let us return to the kind proprietors of Nenaradova, and see what is going on there.

Nothing.

The old people awoke, and went into the sitting-room, Gavril in a night-cap and flannel jacket, Praskovia in a wadded dressing-gown. The samovar was brought in, and, Gavril sent the little maid to ask Maria how she was and how she had slept. The little maid returned, saying that her young lady had slept badly, but that she was better now, and that she would come into the sitting-room in a moment.

And indeed the door opened, and Maria came in and wished her papa and mamma good morning.

"How is your head-ache, Maria?" inquired Gavril.

"Better, papa; answered Maria.

"The fumes from the stoves must have given you your

head-ache," remarked Praskovia.

"Perhaps so, mamma," replied Maria.

The day passed well enough, but in the night Maria was taken ill. A doctor was sent for from town. He came towards evening and found the patient delirious. Soon she was in a severe fever, and in a fortnight the poor patient was on the brink of the grave.

No member of the family knew anything of the flight from home. The letters written by Maria the evening before had been burnt; and the maid, fearing the wrath of the master and mistress, had not breathed a word. The priest, the ex-cornet, the big moustached surveyor, and the little lancer were equally discreet, and with good reason. Tereshka, the coachman, never said too much, not even in his drink. Thus the secret was kept better than it might have been by half a dozen conspirators.

But Maria herself, in the course of her long

fever, let out her secret, nevertheless, her words were so disconnected that her mother, who never left her bedside, could only make out from them that her daughter was desperately in love with Vladimir, and that probably love was the cause of her illness. She consulted her husband and some of her neighbours, and at last it was decided unanimously that the fate of Maria ought not to be interfered with, that a woman must not ride away from the man she is destined to marry, that poverty is no crime, that a woman has to live not with money but with a man, and so on. Moral proverbs are wonderfully useful on such occasions, when we can invent little or nothing in our own justification.

Meanwhile the young lady began to recover. Vladimir had not been seen for a long time in the house of Gravril, so frightened had he been by his previous reception. It was now resolved to send and announce to him the good news which he could scarcely expect: the consent of her parents to his marriage with Maria.

But what was the astonishment of the proprietors of Nenaradova when, in answer to their invitation, they received an insane reply. Vladimir informed them he could never set foot in their house, and begged them to forget an unhappy man whose only hope now was in death. A few days afterwards they heard that Vladimir had left the place and joined the army.

A long time passed before they ventured to tell Maria, who was now recovering. She never mentioned Vladimir.

Some months later, however, finding his name in the list of those who had distinguished themselves and been severely wounded at Borodino, she fainted, and it was feared that the fever might return. But, Heaven be thanked! the fainting fit had no bad results.

*   *   *   *

Maria experienced yet another sorrow. Her father died, leaving her the heiress of all his property. But the inheritance could not console her. She shared sincerely the affliction of her mother, and vowed she would never leave her.

Suitors clustered round the charming

heiress; but she gave no one the slightest hope. Her mother sometimes tried to persuade her to choose a companion in life; but Maria shook her head, and grew pensive.

Vladimir no longer existed. He had died at Moscow on the eve of the arrival of the French. His memory was held sacred by Maria, and she treasured up everything that would remind her of him; books he had read, drawings which he had made; songs he had sung, and the pieces of poetry which he had copied out for her.

The neighbours, hearing all this, wondered at her fidelity, and awaited with curiosity the arrival of the hero who must in the end triumph over the melancholy constancy of this virgin Artemis.

Meanwhile, the war had been brought to a glorious conclusion, and our armies were returning from abroad. The people ran to meet them. The music played, by the regimental bands consisted of war songs, "Vive Henri-Quatre," Tirolese waltzes and airs from Joconde. Nourished on the atmosphere of winter, officers who had started on the campaign mere striplings returned grown men, and covered with decorations. The soldiers conversed gaily among themselves, mingling

German and French words every moment in their speech. A time never to be forgotten--a time of glory and delight! How quickly beat the Russian heart at the words, "Native land!" How sweet the tears of meeting! With what unanimity did we combine feelings of national pride with love for the Tsar! And for him, what a moment!

The women--our Russian women--were splendid then. Their usual coldness disappeared. Their delight was really intoxicating when, meeting the conquerors, they cried, "Hurrah!" And they threw up their caps in the air.

Who of the officers

of that period does not own that to the Russian women he was indebted for his best and most valued reward? During this brilliant period Maria was living with her mother in retirement, and neither of them saw how, in both the capitals, the returning troops were welcomed. But in the districts and villages the general enthusiasm was, perhaps, even greater.

In these places the appearance of an officer became for him a veritable triumph. The accepted lover in plain clothes fared badly by his side.

We have already said that, in spite of her coldness, Maria

was still, as before, surrounded by suitors. But all had to fall in the rear when there arrived at her castle the wounded young colonel of Hussars--Burmin by name--with the order of St. George in his button-hole, and an interesting pallor on his face. He was about twenty-six. He had come home on leave to his estates, which were close to Maria's villa. Maria paid him such attention as none of the others received. In his presence her habitual gloom disappeared. It could not be said that she flirted with him. But a poet, observing her behaviour, might have asked, "S' amor non è, che dunque?"

Burmin was really a very agreeable young

man. He possessed just the kind of sense that pleased women: a sense of what is suitable and becoming. He had no affectation, and was carelessly satirical. His manner towards Maria was simple and easy. He seemed to be of a quiet and modest disposition; but rumour said that he had at one time been terribly wild.

This, however, did not harm him in the opinion of Maria, who (like all other young ladies) excused, with pleasure, vagaries which were the result of impulsiveness and daring.

But above all--more than his love-making, more than his pleasant talk, more than his interesting pallor, more even than his bandaged arm--the silence of the young Hussar excited her curiosity and her imagination. She could not help confessing to herself that he pleased her very much. Probably he too, with his acuteness and his experience, had seen that he interested her. How was it, then, that up to this moment she had not seen

him at her feet; had
not received from
him any declaration
whatever? And
wherefore did she
not encourage him
with more attention,
and, according to
circumstances, even
with tenderness?
Had she a secret of
her own which would
account for her
behaviour?

At last, Burmin

fell into such deep meditation, and his black eyes rested with such fire upon Maria, that the decisive moment seemed very near. The neighbours spoke of the marriage as an accomplished fact, and kind Praskovia rejoiced that her daughter had at last found for herself a worthy mate.

The lady was sitting alone once in the drawing-room, laying out grande-patience, when Burmin entered the room, and at once inquired for Maria.

"She is in the garden," replied the old lady: "go to her, and I will wait for you here." Burmin went, and the old lady made the sign of the cross and thought, "Perhaps the affair will be settled to-day!"

Burmin found Maria in the ivy-bower beside the pond, with a book in her hands, and wearing a white dress--a veritable heroine of romance. After the first inquiries, Maria purposely let the conversation drop; increasing by these

means the mutual
embarrassment,
from which it was
only possible to
escape by means of
a sudden and positive
declaration.

It happened thus.
Burmin, feeling
the awkwardness
of his position,
informed Maria that
he had long sought
an opportunity of
opening his heart

to her, and that he begged for a moment's attention. Maria closed the book and lowered her eyes, as a sign that she was listening.

"I love you," said Burmin, "I love you passionately!" Maria blushed, and bent her head still lower.

"I have behaved imprudently, yielding

as I have done to the seductive pleasure of seeing and hearing you daily." Maria recollected the first letter of St. Preux in 'La Nouvelle Héloïse.'

"It is too late now to resist my fate. The remembrance of you, your dear incomparable image, must from to-day be at once the torment and the consolation of my existence. I have now a grave duty to perform, a terrible secret to disclose, which will place between us an insurmountable barrier."

"It has always existed!" interrupted Maria; "I could never have been your wife."

"I know," he replied quickly; "I know that

you once loved. But death and three years of mourning may have worked some change. Dear, kind Maria, do not try to deprive me of my last consolation; the idea that you might have consented to make me happy if----. Don't speak, for God's sake don't speak--you torture me. Yes, I know, I feel that you could have been mine, but--I am the most miserable of beings--I am already married!"

Maria looked at him in astonishment.

"I am married," continued Burmin; "I have been married more than three years, and do not know who my wife is, or where she is, or whether I shall ever see her again."

"What are you saying?" exclaimed Maria; "how strange! Pray continue."

"In the beginning of 1812," said Burmin, a I was hurrying on to Wilna, where my regiment was stationed. Arriving one evening late at a station, I ordered, the horses to be got ready quickly, when suddenly a fearful snowstorm broke out. Both station master and drivers advised me to wait till it was over. I listened to their advice, but an unaccountable restlessness took possession of me, just as though someone was pushing me on. Meanwhile, the snowstorm did not abate. I could bear it no longer, and again ordered the horses, and started in the midst of the storm. The driver took it into his head to drive along the river, which would shorten the distance by three miles. The banks were covered with snowdrifts; the driver missed the turning which would have brought us out on to the road, and we turned up in an unknown place. The storm never ceased. I could discern a light, and told the driver to make for it. We entered a village, and found that the light proceeded from a wooden church. The church was open. Outside the railings stood several sledges, and people passing in and out through the porch.

"'Here! here!' cried several voices. I told the coachman to drive up.

"'Where have you dawdled?' said someone to me. 'The bride has fainted; the priest does not know what to do: we were on the point of going back. Make haste and get out!'

"I got out of the

sledge in silence, and stepped into the church, which was dimly lighted with two or three tapers. A girl was sitting in a dark corner on a bench; and another girl was rubbing her temples. 'Thank God,' said the latter, 'you have come at last! You have nearly been the death of the young lady.'

"The old priest approached me; saying,

"'Shall I begin?'

"'Begin--begin, reverend father,' I replied, absently.

"The young lady was raised up. I thought her rather pretty. Oh, wild, unpardonable frivolity! I placed myself by her side at the altar. The priest hurried on.

"Three men and the maid supported the bride, and occupied themselves with her alone. We were married!

"'Kiss your wife,' said the priest.

"My wife turned her pale face towards me. I was going to

kiss her, when she exclaimed, 'Oh! it is not he--not he!' and fell back insensible.

"The witnesses stared at me. I turned round and left the church without any attempt being made to stop me, threw myself into the sledge, and cried, 'Away!'"

"What!" exclaimed

Maria. "And you don't know what became of your unhappy wife?"

"I do not," replied Burmin; "neither do I know the name of the village where I was married, nor that of the station from which I started. At that time I thought so little of my wicked joke that, on driving away from the church, I fell asleep, and never woke till early the next morning, after reaching the third station. The servant who was with me died during the campaign, so that I have now no hope of ever discovering the unhappy woman on whom I played such a cruel trick, and who is now so cruelly avenged."

"Great heavens!"

cried Maria, seizing his hand. "Then it was you, and you do not recognise me?" Burmin turned pale--and threw himself at her feet.

THE END

ABOUT THE AUTHOR

Alexander Pushkin was a poet, playwright, and novelist of the Romantic era who is considered by many to be the greatest Russian poet and the founder of modern Russian literature. He died after being shot in a duel with a Frenchman who had wooed his wife.

ABOUT THE COVER

The cover is adapted from a painting by Cornelius Krieghoff from 1860, called The Blizzard.

MORE CLASSIC TITLES AVAILABLE IN SUPER LARGE PRINT

* The Bohemian Girl *
Willa Cather
When Nils left the farm, he said goodbye to his mother, brother and sweetheart Clara. Now he's returned but for love or obligation?

* The Lady Rustic *
Alexander Pushkin

* Her Hero *
Ethel M. Dell
Another delightful tale from the titan of feel good romances. She is at her finest in this story fit for an episode of Downton Abbey.

* The Man with Two Left Feet *
P.G. Wodehouse

* All Cats Are Gray *
Andre Norton

* White Fang *
Jack London

* Beethoven *
Romain Rolland

* Gettysburg *
Frederick Tillberg

* Abraham Lincoln's Greatest Speeches *

* Selections from the King James Bible *

ROMANCE
ADVENTURE
MYSTERY
THRILLER
HORROR
SCIENCE FICTION
FANTASY
POETRY
HUMOR
HISTORY
BIOGRAPHY
MEMOIR

it's all available in...
SUPER LARGE PRINT

WHAT WE'RE ABOUT

I started making Super Large Print books for my own grandma, so she wouldn't have to stop reading books when large print wasn't big enough anymore. Since she was a little girl, my grandma had delighted in reading but also in the tactile joy of turning pages and holding a beloved book in her hands. She didn't want to give up the pleasures of the page just because her vision had diminished. Books are friends we should get to keep as long as possible. I hope these books will be welcome companions to others who want to keep on reading real books.

You can learn more at superlargeprint.com

MORE BOOKS AT:
superlargeprint.com

KEEP ON READING!

ISBN 1985317397
ISBN 978-1985317390

Made in the USA
Coppell, TX
15 November 2020